Two Hearts

A story based on history

Second Edition

Tana Reiff

Illustrations by Tyler Stiene

PRO LINGUA ASSOCIATES

Pro Lingua Associates, Publishers

P.O. Box 1348
Brattleboro, Vermont 05302-1348 USA
Office: 802 257 7779
Orders: 800 366 4775
E-mail: orders@ProLinguaAssociates.com
SAN: 216-0579
Webstore: www.ProLinguaAssociates.com

Text ISBN 13: 978-0-86647-426-9; 10: 0-86647-426-9
Audio CD ISBN 13: 978-0-86647-427-6; 10: 0-86647-427-7

The first edition of this book was originally published by Fearon Education, a division of David S. Lake Publishers, Belmont, California, Copyright © 1989, later by Pearson Education. This, the second edition, has been revised and redesigned.

The cover and illustrations are by Tyler Stiene. The book was set and designed by Tana Reiff, consulting with A.A. Burrows, using the Adobe *Century Schoolbook* typeface for the text. This is a digital adaptation of one of the most popular faces of the twentieth century. Century's distinctive roman and italic fonts and its clear, dark strokes and serifs were designed, as the name suggests, to make schoolbooks easy to read. The display font used on the cover and titles is a 21st-century digital invention titled Telugu. It is designed to work on all digital platforms and with Indic scripts. Telugu is named for the Telugu people in southern India and their widely spoken language. This is a simple, strong, and interesting sans serif display font.

This book was printed and bound by KC Book Manufacturing in North Kansas City, Missouri. Printed in the United States. Second Edition, Second Printing 2018

The Hopes and Dreams Series
by Tana Reiff

The Magic Paper (Mexican-Americans)
For Gold and Blood (Chinese-Americans)
Nobody Knows (African-Americans)
Little Italy (Italian-Americans)
Hungry No More (Irish-Americans)
Sent Away (Japanese-Americans)
Two Hearts (Greek-Americans)

Contents

1 Adonia Needs a Husband

A Mountain Village in Greece, 1910

"We are poor as dirt,"
said George Stavros's mother.
"And you are too young
to make money.
Our only hope
is for your sister
to get a good husband.
But how do we find
a good husband for her?
We have no dowry.
No gift of money
for a man.
Your father is dead.
And Greece
is in a sorry state.
Many men
are out of work.
So what can we do?"

George's sister Adonia
was dark and pretty.

But being pretty
was not as important
as having money.
And the more money
a family had,
the better the husband
a young woman
might get.

"Poor Adonia,"
said Mama.
"Look at her."

George's sister
sat by the one window
of the little house.
"Maybe I could find
a good man,
even without a dowry,"
she said.

"You dream,"
said Mama.
"I have high hopes
for my children.
You will not marry
just any man
who comes along."

Mama rocked
in her chair.
Like all Greek widows
she wore only black.
She would wear black
until the day she died.
She was only 40 years old.
She had no hope
of having another husband
of her own.
Her only hope
was for her children.

George began to sing.
I want to go
to far away lands.
To far away lands
I must go.

"What is this song?"
Mama asked.

"It's about America,"
said George.
"All the boys
sing this song.
In fact, Mama,
a man spoke
with some of us boys.

He has jobs for us
in America.
I can go there
and make money
for Adonia's dowry."

Mama looked George
right in the face.
"You mean to tell me
Greek boys can go
to a far away land
for work?"
Mama thought
for just a moment.
Then she said,
"I will tell you
what I think.
George, you should go
to America.
Send us money
for your sister.
We will be all right
until you come home."

But when the day came
for George to leave,
Mama was not so ready
to see him go.

There were tears
in her eyes
as George kissed her goodbye.

The boys walked
in a line
down the mountain.
Each boy
carried a heavy pack
on his back.

George turned around
for one more look
at the village.
The little houses
were tiny white boxes
against the green mountain.
He could see
the open fields
high up the mountain.
There he had watched
a little herd of goats.
George would never forget
those happy days.
He did not want to leave.
This was home.
The mountain.
The village.

The country of Greece.
George wondered
if he would ever again
see anything so beautiful.
Yet he couldn't wait
to make a good dowry
for dear Adonia.

At the bottom
of the mountain
George picked up
a little, round, gray stone.
He put it
in his pocket.
There it stayed,
for the whole trip
to America.

2 The Shoeshine Boy

When George and his friends
set foot in New York,
some men met them
at Ellis Island.
"Come with me,"
said one man to George.
"I am your padrone.
I will take you
to your job."
He tipped
his round, black hat.

He took George
to a busy street
deep in the busy city.
They turned down
a little side street.
They went inside
one of the buildings.
George followed the man
up the stairs,
up five floors.

They walked
to a room
at the end
of a dark hall.

"You will sleep there."
The padrone
pointed to a bed.
"With two other boys.
Two beds.
Six boys.
Not so bad!"

George was afraid
to say anything.
All he did
was look away.
He had never lived
in a place like this.
The room
had two beds
and nothing more.
It smelled bad.
There was no window.
The beds
had no sheets,
just rough old blankets.

"All right, then,"
said the padrone.
"Now I will show you
where you will work."

Out on the street again,
George took a deep breath.
The air
did not smell clean
like the mountain air
back home.
But it was better than
that little room.
He walked
behind the padrone
to the next block.
The padrone stopped
at a bootblack shop.

"You will
shine shoes here,"
he told George.
"Meet your boss.
This is Kostas.
This is his shop.
You will work here.
Kostas will feed you.

Now I will go.
I'll stop back soon
and check on you.
Good day!"
The padrone
tipped his black hat
and left the shop.

"Now watch me,"
Kostas said.
"I will show you
how to do
a perfect spitshine!"
The boy watched
as Kostas
ran the shoeshine rag
over the shoe.
He made the rag
fly back and forth.
George wondered
how he could ever work
as fast as Kostas.

But each day,
George worked faster
than the day before.
Men in suits came by
from 6:00 a.m. to 9:00 p.m.

George shined
their shoes and boots
until he could see
his own face
in the toes.
To pass the time,
he tried to understand
people speaking English.
Every day
the padrone came by
to pick up the boy's tips.
Every night
George went to his room.
His arms, neck, and back ached.

But Kostas said,
"Why do they send me
lazy boys like you?"

"I try very hard,"
said George.

"You and I—
we're stuck
with each other,"
said Kostas.
"And don't try
to run away!

Heaven only knows
what your padrone
would do to you.
So get on the stick!
Work better!
Work faster!"

The one good part
of George's life
was making friends
with an older boy
in the shop.

"When do we get paid?"
George asked Gus
after a few months
on the job.

"I get paid
next month,"
Gus said.
"20 dollars
for the year!
You won't get a cent
until you finish
your first year here."

"No pay for a year?"
George asked.

"That's the deal,"
said Gus.

"I came here
to make money
for my sister's dowry,"
said George.
"Now I'm stuck
in this bootblack shop."
He was almost crying.

"You're not stuck,"
said Gus.
"You can walk out
anytime you wish."

"Why don't you leave?"
George asked Gus.

"I'd have to find
a place to live,"
said Gus.
"The padrones
are not kind people.
But they do keep
a roof over our heads.
Put in some time here
and it pays off."

George didn't feel good
about any of this news.
He couldn't see himself
waiting a whole year
to get paid.
He was only a boy,
and he felt very alone.
He didn't feel ready
to be on his own
in a strange country.

Then an old friend
from his village
told him about a restaurant
in the city.
It would be easy
to get work there.

The next day,
George didn't show up
for work.
He headed downtown.
He walked
into the restaurant
and never returned
to the bootblack shop.

3 A Restaurant Job

The sign
on the restaurant window
read, **HELP WANTED**.
George knew
just enough English
to read that.

He walked inside
and found the owner.
"You have work here?"
he asked in English.

"Speak-y English, huh?"
laughed Mr. Carter.
"No matter.
No need to speak
to clear tables!
But I can't take you on
in those clothes."

George saw himself
in the window.

His clothes
were almost rags.
One empty pocket
hung out of his pants.

"I'll tell you what,"
said Mr. Carter.
"I have rooms upstairs.
Running water, too.
I will pay you
a little less each week
and you can live up there."

George's face lit up.
He understood
what Mr. Carter
was saying.

"Now go upstairs
and clean yourself up,"
said Mr. Carter.
He threw
a white shirt and pants
into George's open arms.
"Put on these clothes
and come back downstairs.
I need a busboy
right away."

So once again George
was working long hours
for low pay.
But he got paid
once a week,
not once a year.
Every day
he thanked Mr. Carter
for giving him a job.
And every month
he sent home
a little money
for Adonia's dowry.

"This is great!"
he often said to himself.
"Come to America
and get work!
Make money!
Send money home
to Greece!"

Then one day
George got a letter
from his mother.
"You must come home,"
she wrote.

"There's a war here.
Greece needs our young men
to fight the Turks."*

There was no question
in George's mind.
He had to help Greece.
He *wanted* to help Greece.
He boarded a ship
back to the old country.
But he was sick
in his heart.
He was going back
without a dowry
for Adonia.
And not a penny
in his pocket.
Only a little, round, gray stone.
And a pocket
full of dreams.

----

*In the two Balkan Wars of 1912 and
1913, Greece and its allies, Bulgaria,
Serbia, and Montenegro, defeated Turkey.
Then Bulgaria turned on its allies, but it
was defeated.

4 Second Time Around

And so, in 1912,
George Stavros
was back in Greece.
A little older now,
he joined the army.
By the next year,
the fighting was over.

Once again,
men came to the village
looking for young men
to work in America.
George needed work.
Adonia still needed a husband.
Mama said
that George should go.

This time,
George went to Chicago
to work in a factory.
His job
was to put pieces
into machines.

He stood up all day long
as each machine
came down the line.
He had to be quick
and watch out
for his fingers.
He hated
every minute of it.
He hated
spending all day
in a hot factory.

George lived
in a large house
with other young men
from his village.
The house
was in Chicago's Greektown.
George was happy
to have work and friends.
But this life
was really not much
to be happy about.

Things changed
when a new church
was built in Greektown.
Now there was
a place to go.

George and his friends
could pray and sing together,
just like in Greece.
There were dinners
of lamb and salad
and Greek pastries.
And young women
to get to know.

George always knew
he would marry
a Greek woman.
He did not know
that he would meet her
in America.
Her name was Daphne.
He met her
at a church dinner.

It was love
at first sight.
As soon as he saw her
he knew she was the one.
For days after the dinner
he could think of nothing
but Daphne.
Beautiful Daphne.

He saw her again
the next Sunday
at church.
She looked at George
the same way
he looked at her.
She smiled at him
the same way
he smiled at her.
Hundreds of people
filled the church.
But for George and Daphne
there were only two.

One day
George and Daphne
were walking in the park.
"Wouldn't it be nice
if we were married?"
said Daphne.

George stopped
in his tracks.
Nothing would be better
than to marry Daphne.
But that was not possible.

"We cannot marry
until I make
my sister's dowry,"
George said softly.
"And I have
a long way to go.
Then I will return
to Greece.
That is the plan."

"I understand,"
said Daphne.
"You know,
I have no dowry
to give to you.
We don't have dowries
in America."

But as months went by
George began to believe
that he could not stay
at the factory.

"It looks as if
I must return home early,"
he told Daphne.

"Can't you find
other work here?"
she asked.

"Well, I do have
one idea,"
George began.
"It might be fun
to buy a pushcart.
I could sell ice cream
on the street.
I'd be outside
all day long."

"Selling ice cream!
That's a fine idea!"
said Daphne.
"Will you give me
free ice cream?"

"Of course!"
said George.
"I will give you
all the ice cream
in the world!"

5 Selling Ice Cream

One day,
Daphne was walking
down the street.
She spotted a sign
in a restaurant window:
PUSHCART FOR SALE.

"I started
with that pushcart,"
the owner told her.
"Now I have
a whole restaurant!"

Daphne hurried off
to tell George.
"Maybe you could
do the same thing!"
she said to him.
"Start with a pushcart.
Then open a restaurant!"

"One thing at a time!"
George laughed.

He bought the pushcart
for a few dollars
each month
until it was paid for.
He put a block of ice
in the wagon.
He put tubs of ice cream
on the ice.
He bought
a big white and blue umbrella
for the pushcart.
And he painted
ICE CREAM
on three sides
of the cart.
Then he pushed it
along the streets.
On hot days
he pushed it
all the way
to the lake.

"Ice cream! Ice cream!
Five cents a dish!"
he called out.
Everybody loved ice cream.

Almost everybody
bought ice cream
from George.
He counted the money
every night,
and smiled.

One morning
he pushed his cart
to his favorite spot.
Much to his surprise,
another man and pushcart
were already there.

"Hey, this spot is mine!"
George called to the man.
"What are you doing here?"

"Selling hot dogs,"
the man answered.

"Find your own spot!"
said George.

"I'm doing fine
right where I am,"
said the man.

George put up his hands.
He was angry enough
to start a fight.
"You had better move!"
he shouted.

"Hot dogs and ice cream
are two different things,"
said the man.
"We both
can work this spot."

So they did.
Ice cream and hot dogs
in one place.
But pushcarts have wheels.
So, seven days a week
both carts
moved around the city
as pushcarts do.
Sometimes people
found them both
at the same spot –
ice cream and hot dogs.

6 Time to Marry

Two years later
George still sold ice cream
on the street.
Now he sold it
in sugar cones
with nuts on top.

Daphne still waited
to marry George.
Back in Greece,
Adonia still waited
for a husband too,
even though she had a dowry.
George had finally
sent home enough money
for a fine dowry.
Ice cream money,
he called it.
But most of the men
of the village
had gone to America
or were killed
in the wars.

"Now what do I do?"
George said to Daphne.
"My sister
has a dowry.
I have done my duty
for her.
But how can I
return to Greece
when I am making money
here in America?"

"What do you
want to do?"
Daphne asked him.

"I want to find
a little store
in Greektown,"
said George.
"I want to start
an ice cream shop!
I can't do that
back in Greece."

"Then do it here,"
said Daphne.
"I will help you."

"I also want
to marry you,"
George added.
"I make enough money
for both of us
to live on.
What do you say?"

Daphne threw her arms
around George.
"Of course,
I'll marry you!
I'll tell my parents!
We will have
a big Greek wedding!"

"Good! Good!"
George said.
"First we will marry.
Then we will start
our ice cream shop."

"Wait a minute,"
said Daphne.
"I will marry you
only if the shop
is closed on Sundays."

"I sell
a lot of ice cream
on Sundays,"
said George.

"No Sundays,"
said Daphne
with her arms crossed.
"Church and family
are more important
than money."

"Very well,"
said George.
"No Sundays."

George and Daphne
got married
in the new church.
Everyone in Greektown
was welcome.

"There must be
400 people here!"
George whispered to Daphne
as they danced
at their wedding.

"I say 500!"
laughed Daphne.
"And most of them
brought along
homemade Greek food!"

"It is all wonderful,"
said George.
"Now, I've been thinking.
What kinds of ice cream
should we sell
in our shop?"

"Can't you ever
take your mind off business?"
Daphne asked.
She wasn't really angry.
She was as ready as George
to open the shop.

Not long
after the wedding,
they opened the shop.
It was a tiny space
that opened
onto the street.

There was room
for one freezer
full of ice cream.
There was room
for two or three people
to stand at the counter
and order a favorite flavor.
There were no tables.
Just ice cream,
hungry people,
George, Daphne,
and a money box.

But the only thing
that felt crowded
was the money box.
It filled up fast.
George had to go
to the bank
three times a day.

The first few weeks,
two signs hung
in the window.
One said: ICE CREAM.
The other said:
PUSHCART FOR SALE.

Then one day
a young man
from Greece
bought the old pushcart.

 George took down
the pushcart sign.
That was the day he knew
he had two hearts.
One heart
was still back in Greece.
Now the other
would stay in America.

7 A Growing Business

Over the next few years
George and Daphne
had three children.
They named the two girls
Phoebe and Myra.
The boy
was named Andreas,
after George's father.
They called him Andy
for short.

As soon as the children
began to walk
they were helping out
in the ice cream shop.
They could say
"vanilla" and "chocolate"
before they could say
their own names.

All the customers said,
"What sweet children!"

"We start them
working young around here,"
Daphne would laugh.

Of the three children,
Andy took
the most interest
in the business.
By the time
he was six years old
he was scooping ice cream.
By the time
he was 14 years old
he was working
as much as his parents.
By the time
he was 16
he asked to be paid.
By the time
he was 18
he had his own ideas
for running the business.
Sometimes he forgot
that his father
was the boss,
in both the family
and the business.

"Bamba, don't you think
it's time for this business
to grow?"
Andy asked his father
one day.

"What do you mean?"
George asked his son.
"We make a good living.
You children
never go hungry.
What do you mean, grow?"

"Well, some people
who come in here
ask me why
we don't have tables,"
said Andy.
"I say to them,
'Where would we put tables?'
Anyone can see
there's not enough room
to turn around in here."

"What's wrong
with that?"
asked George.

"Well, I was thinking,"
Andy started.
"We should find
a bigger shop
that will fit tables."

"That sounds to me
like a restaurant,"
said George.

"That's the idea!"
said Andy.
"Let's turn our business
into a restaurant!"

"Let me think about that,"
said George.

Andy was surprised
when a few days later
his father said,
"I've been thinking.
Let's open
a little restaurant."
George made it sound
like his own idea.

"Great idea, Bamba!"
said Andy.
"A place down the street
is for rent right now.
Let's take a look."

8 **Running a Restaurant**

George knew about
the restaurant business
from his days
in New York.
He planned
his own restaurant
in every way.
He was the one
who decided
where each table
should go.
He was the one
who decided
what color
the tablecloths should be.
He was the one
who decided
what foods
should be on the menu.
He was the one
who decided
how much cheese
to put in the spinach pie.

Everything here
was done George's way.
The whole family
worked in the restaurant.
But no one but George
made the decisions.
That's why
the restaurant's name
was "George's."

So when Andy
married Cleo,
George was not ready
for one more person
in the family business.
He surely wasn't ready
for Cleo.

Andy's new wife
was a beautiful Greek-American.
She also was a person
not afraid to speak her mind.
"So this is your restaurant,"
she said to Andy
the first time she saw it.
"Why in the world
are the tablecloths green?"

"Bamba says
green makes him think
of the mountains
back in Greece,"
Andy explained.

"The tablecloths
should be red,"
said Cleo.
"No question about it.
Red makes people hungry."

That's how things went
when Cleo was around.
No matter how well
things were going,
Cleo always had
a better idea.

"You should tell your wife
who's boss around here,"
George whispered to Andy.
"In Greece,
no woman
would get away with
the things Cleo says."

"This isn't Greece,"
said Andy.

"I know that,"
said George.
"But we are Greek.
Greek men
are in charge.
I'm in charge
of this restaurant.
You're in charge
of your wife.
Understand, son?"

"There's no stopping Cleo,"
said Andy.
"She's a strong woman."

"Well, if you ask me,
She should keep her ideas
to herself,"
said George.

"That's enough, Bamba,"
said Andy.
"I'll talk to Cleo.

She's a member
of the family now.
I want the two of you
to get along."

   That night
Andy had a talk
with Cleo.
"You have to understand
the way Bamba
was brought up,"
said Andy.
"In his way of thinking,
men come first."

   "This is a man
who came to America
to give his sister
a dowry,"
Cleo laughed.
"Listen, Andy.
I was raised
by Greek parents too.
They taught me a lot
about the restaurant business.
I do know
what I'm talking about."

"I know you do,"
said Andy.
"But can you try
not to make Bamba
so angry?
Make him think
your ideas
are his ideas?"

"I'll work on it,"
said Cleo.
"I love your father.
He just doesn't know it yet."

9 A Trip to Greece

George and Cleo
got along better
in the years
that followed.
They still had some fights
over how to run things, however.
So when George said
that he and Daphne
were going on a trip,
Cleo was glad.
She was sure
that a little space
between her and George
would be good for everyone.

"Your mama and I
are going to Greece!"
George told the family.
"I can't stay away
any longer!
I must see my home again
before I die."

Cleo looked at Andy
and rolled her eyes.
"All these years here
and he still doesn't
call Chicago home?"
she whispered.

Andy shook his head.
"You and I
were born here,"
he said.
"Chicago is
the only home
we know.
Remember,
Bamba came here
with the idea
of going back someday.
He's done well here.
But he still loves Greece."

"We will leave
on Friday morning,"
George went on.
"Phoebe and Myra
will drive us
to the airport.

Cleo, you keep an eye
on the house
while we are away.
Andy, you run the restaurant.
And all of you,
you must go to church
every Sunday!
The big Greek dinner
is coming up.
I want everyone
to help out."

Cleo rolled her eyes again.
"Why am I the one
to watch the house?
You have two sisters,"
she whispered to Andy.

"He's probably afraid
you'll change something
at the restaurant,"
said Andy.
"Don't worry.
I need your help
to run the place."

So George and Daphne
took a trip to Greece.
When George saw
the old village again,
everything seemed the same—
at first.
The little houses
still looked
like tiny white boxes
against the green mountains.
Everything
was still beautiful.
Yet something
felt very different.
George just couldn't
put his finger on what.

Mama was gone now,
but Adonia lived
in the old place.
That was different
from the old days.

Both times
he had left here,
he was a boy, really.

Now he was a man
with a family
of his own.
He had a life
of his own
in America.
That was different
from the old days.

George and Daphne
were not rich,
but they were well off.
They owned a business,
a nice house,
and two cars.
That was different
from the old days.

Still, George
could not put his finger
on what felt different here.

George, Daphne, and Adonia
visited places in Greece
that none of them
had ever seen before.

They went to the islands
and rode in a little boat
with a white sail.
They went to Athens
and saw the great old buildings
they only had seen pictures of.
But the city of Athens
was crowded and dirty.
"Chicago is much nicer
than this!"
George said.

When they returned
to the village,
George wasn't talking.

"What's the matter?"
asked Daphne.
"This isn't like you."

"We have visited
all these beautiful places,"
said George.
"But that's just it.
It's a visit.

I am ready
to return to Chicago.
I want to get back
to my family and business."

   Daphne smiled
at her husband.
"I feel the same way,"
she said.
"Greece has had
wars and hard times.
Still, in many ways,
it has not changed
over the years.
But you have.
You are a man
of two hearts,
George Stavros.
One of those hearts
has found a home
in America."

10 Red Tablecloths

George and Daphne
were away for two months.
Back in Chicago,
the first thing George did
was go to the restaurant.
He was very surprised
at what he found there.

When he walked in
he was sure
he was in the wrong restaurant.
The tablecloths were red.
Then he heard Andy's voice.
"Bamba, you're home!"

"What's going on here?"
George asked his son.

Just then Cleo
stepped out of the kitchen.
"I waited ten years
to change those tablecloths,"
she said.
"I hope you like them."

"To tell the truth,
I do like them,"
George said.
"They make the place
nice and bright.
Did you change
the menu too?"

Andy handed George
a new, red menu.
George opened it up.
"What's this?
Fried chicken?
Hamburgers?
PIZZA?!
This is a Greek restaurant!
Not American!
Not Italian!
What have you done
to my restaurant?"

"People want
more than Greek food,"
Andy said.
He pulled out a paper
to show his father.
"Look at these numbers, Bamba!

We did more business
in the last two months
than any two months ever!"

"Good numbers,"
said George
without looking up.
Then he raised his head
and pounded his chest.
"You have cut me
to the heart!
I go away
and you take over
my restaurant!
I will never go away again!"

"Can't you be happy
we take an interest
in the business?"
Cleo asked.
But George
did not look happy.

The next morning
George did not show up
at the restaurant.
"Bamba must be very angry,"
said Andy.

Then, at noon,
George walked in.
"Big news, everyone!"
he called out.
"I just signed a lease!
I am going to open
a new Greek restaurant!"

"Are you crazy?"
Andy asked his father.

"You bet I'm crazy!"
said George.
"Crazy like a fox!
You two
can run this restaurant.
Your mother and I
will run the new one."

"What about
Phoebe and Myra?"
Andy asked.

"Phoebe would rather
go to school
all her life,"
said George.

"Myra and her husband
are running
their movie house.
The rest of us
are the restaurant people.
Now, what did you do
with those old green menus
and green tablecloths?
I need them
for the new place."

11 A Chain of Restaurants

George's new restaurant
did well from the start.
Most of the people
who ate there
were not Greek.
For these people,
Greek food
was new and different.

With the new place,
George got along better
with Andy and Cleo.
One day Andy said,
"Bamba, I'm ready
to open another restaurant.
Why don't we
do it together?"

"Greek or American?"
George wanted to know.

"I'm thinking Italian,"
said Andy.
"I'm thinking pizza.

We sell a whole lot
of pizza
at the old place."

George laughed.
"Everybody loves pizza!
Why not?"

"We can open
one this year,
one next year,"
said Andy.
"Maybe another one
the year after that.
We'll be
all over town.
A chain!"

"I like it,"
George said,
nodding his head.

Andy smiled.
He couldn't believe
that his father
liked his idea.
He couldn't believe
that his father
hadn't made it sound
like his own idea.

"Great, Bamba!"
was all he said.

"What will we call
the new chain?"
George asked.

"He's asking me
what to name
the new restaurants,"
Andy thought to himself.

But George
had his own idea.
"I have
just the right name,"
he said.
"George's Pizza!"

"Of course!"
said Andy.
"No better name
in the world!"

Andy shook
his father's hand.
"We've come a long way
from ice cream,
haven't we, Bamba?"

12 Soft Hearts

   With George's Pizza
George had never been so busy.
He was having a ball.
And it was nice
to work with Andy,
and even Cleo.

   Everything was perfect.
But then Daphne
got sick.
The doctors said
it was cancer.
They did
all they could for her.
But in just six months
she took her last breath.

   George's heart
was broken.
His dear Daphne
was gone.

He didn't know
what to do
with himself.
So he spent
all of his time
running the restaurants.
He hopped
from one to another.
He kept them running
like a well-oiled machine.

But George Stavros
was not a young man now.
All the work,
all the running around,
was starting to wear on him.

One morning
he was having trouble
getting out of bed.
Slowly, he set one foot
on the floor.
Then the other foot.
He felt as if
he might fall over.
So he called
his doctor.

"I'll see you
at the hospital,"
said the doctor.
"An ambulance
is on the way."

George was rushed
to the hospital.
"You have had
a mild heart attack,"
the doctor told him.
"You must take it easy
for a few months."

"Me, take it easy?"
laughed George.
"You must be kidding!"

"I'm not kidding,"
said the doctor.
"You were lucky this time.
But if you don't
rest and slow down,
one more heart attack
could kill you."

Andy and Cleo
came to visit him
that night.

"What will I do?"
George asked them.
"Who will take care of me?
Phoebe took that teaching job
in North Carolina.
Myra and her family
are all tied up
with their movie house.
I will not go
to a nursing home.
That's not the Greek way."

Neither Andy nor Cleo
made a sound.
Then Cleo
began to speak.
"I'll take care of you,"
she said.
George had never heard her
speak in such a sweet voice.
It was full of love
he had never heard
from his daughter-in-law.

"You?" George asked.

"I mean it, Bamba,"
said Cleo.

"We'll work things out
with the restaurants.
They almost run themselves."
She took George's hand.
"Come and live
with Andy and me."

And so Cleo
took care of George
for the next few months.
Little by little,
George became ready
to go back to work.

The first month at work,
he didn't push himself.
The second month,
he moved a little faster.
By the third month,
George was working
as hard as ever.

One morning
as he pulled up
at the old George's restaurant
he felt a little sick.
He parked his car
and made his way inside.

But as he opened the door,
everything went black.
Without a word,
he fell to the floor
like a rag doll.

Cleo ran to him.
"Bamba! Bamba!"
she cried.
She patted his face.
"Call a doctor!"
she called to a busboy.
"He's out like a light!"

It took ten minutes
before the ambulance came.
"Almost no heartbeat,"
they said.
"We must get him
to the hospital."

Cleo started
to empty his pockets
when Andy walked in.
"Here's his money,"
she said to her husband.
"And his cards.
And what's this?

A little gray stone?"

"Oh, my God!"
said Andy.
"I've seen that stone!
Bamba showed it to me
when I was a child.
It's from Greece.
He brought it with him
the first time
he came to America!"

"He's carried it with him
all these years?"
said Cleo.
"That's really something."

Andy took the stone
in his hand.
"Sometimes Bamba's head
was as hard as this stone,"
he cried.
"But only a man
with a soft heart
would carry a stone
from the old country
all these years."

"That stone
stands for Bamba's Greek heart,"
said Cleo.
"It was always
a part of him."

"Bamba's Greek heart
will always be
part of all of us,"
Andy said.
And with that,
George's son
kissed the little round stone
and put it
in his own pocket.

Glossary

Definitions and examples of certain words and terms used in the story

Chapter 1 — Adonia Needs a Husband page 1

dowry — Money that is paid to a man for marrying a family's daughter.
We have no dowry.

sorry state — In this case, weak or poor condition.
And Greece is in a sorry state.

rocked (to rock) — To move one's body back and forth.
Mama rocked in her chair.

herd — Many animals in a group, usually watched by a person.
There he had watched a little herd of goats.

Chapter 2 — The Shoeshine Boy page 7

shoeshine boy — A boy whose job is to shine people's shoes.

set foot — To arrive, usually for the first time.
*When George and his friends set foot in
New York, some men met them.*

padrone — A man who helps immigrants
find a job. He may take part of their pay.
*I am your padrone. I will take you to
your job.*

tipped (to tip) — To lift one's hat slightly
as a gesture to show good manners or
just to say "hello" or "goodbye."
He tipped his round, black hat.

bootblack shop — A shop where people
bring their boots to be cleaned and
polished.
The padrone stopped at a bootblack shop.

spitshine — A very bright shoeshine. The
shiner may use his spit to increase the
shine.
*I will show you how to do a perfect
spitshine!*

rag — A piece of cloth used for cleaning or
wiping.
He made the rag fly back and forth.

tips — The extra money customers may give to the person who gives a service.
Every day the padrone came by to pick up the boy's tips.

get on the stick — Do better and don't complain.
So get on the stick!

pays off (to pay off) — To have good results from the work you do.
Put in some time here and it pays off.

show up — To appear; to be where you should be.
The next day, George didn't show up for work.

Chapter 3 — The Restaurant Job page 15

No matter — It is not important.
No matter. No need to speak to clear tables!

take you on — To hire someone.
But I can't take you on in those clothes.

busboy — A restaurant worker who clears and cleans the tables.
I need a busboy right away.

Chapter 4 — Second Time Around

in his tracks — Stopping without taking another step forward.
George stopped in his tracks.

pushcart — A small cart with wheels which is moved (pushed) from place to place.
It might be fun to buy a pushcart.

Chapter 5 — Selling Ice Cream

tub — A large container.
He put tubs of ice cream on the ice.

Chapter 6 — Time to Marry

cone — A container for ice cream. It has an open top and closes to a point at the bottom. It can be eaten.
Now he sold it in sugar cones with nuts on top.

Chapter 7 — A Growing Business

scooping (to scoop) — Using a special spoon to cut into the ice cream and shape it into a ball.
By the time he was six year old he was scooping ice cream.

Chapter 8 — Running a Restaurant page 41

running (to run) — To operate and manage a business.

why in the world — "Why" said as a surprise or question.
Why in the world are the tablecloths green?

in charge — Directing; telling others what to do.
Greek men are in charge.

no stopping — Not able to control.
There's no stopping Cleo.

Chapter 9 — A Trip to Greece page 47

got along (to get along) — To work and live together without big problems.
George and Cleo got along better in the years that followed.

rolled (to roll) one's eyes — To move one's eyeballs upward to show disbelief or disagreement.
Cleo looked at Andy and rolled her eyes.

keep an eye on — To watch and take care of something.
Cleo, you keep an eye on the house while we are away.

Chapter 10 — Red Tablecloths page 54

take over — To take control of something.
I go away and you take over my restaurant!

lease — A contract to rent something.
I just signed a lease! I am going to open a new Greek restaurant!

crazy like a fox — smart, clever, not foolish.
You bet I'm crazy! Crazy like a fox!

Chapter 11 — A Chain of Restaurants page 59

chain — Several businesses with one owner. They often look very similar.

nodding (to nod) — To move the head up and down to agree.
"I like it," George said, nodding his head.

Chapter 12 — Soft Hearts page 62

having (to have) a ball — To have a
wonderful time.
*George had never been so busy. He was
having a ball.*

hopped (to hop) — To move suddenly in
short jumps.
He hopped from one to another.

mild — Not strong.
You have had a mild heart attack.

take it easy — Relax; not work so hard.
You must take it easy for a few months.

kidding (to kid) — To joke with or tease
someone.
*"Me, take it easy?" laughed George. "You
must be kidding!"*

nursing home — A place for old people
who cannot care for themselves.
I will not go to a nursing home.

rag doll — A soft doll made of cloth. It is
not stiff.
*Without a word, he fell to the floor like a
rag doll.*